No Bright Shield

George McCauley

SOMETHING MORE PUBLICATIONS

ISBN 0-9622889-0-X

Library of Congress Catalogue Card Number: 89-91756

Printed in the United States of America

The publication of this book is supported
by a grant from the George Link Jr. Foundation, Inc.

For friends, real and imagined, who prompted the muse: Colleen, Chuck, Georgia, Frank, Sir Alec, Bernie and Vera, Lindsay, Pan Michael, Sherry, Beau, John and Digby, Ronnie, Saint Paul, Kate, T.H. White, Vinny O and the Boston Bills.

CONTENTS

Flood Tide

They come like waves,
uneven in enthusiasm
for this foreign strand
where trees stick up
like broken teeth
from the sand and
rocks reef outward
in unyielding welcome.

Some hesitate
before the unfamiliar
shore as though the
lapping sameness
of the sea still holds
them back with promises
of oceanic restfulness
and drifting memories,
of shapeless moon-dreams
on a summer's night.
Some crest proudly
as if to show their
stuff before they're
splayed upon the beach.
Some sigh as they
dissolve into the sultry,
shining bosom of the earth,
her seagreen necklace
strung with different
shapes of shells,

and, well, see them
come, these catechumens,

pouring from the nations
to this christening,
this christendom.

*

They're greeted by a
lusty crew, baptismal
characters each one of
them, old Noah with his
frantic compass and his
soggy maps, a clothespin
on his nose against
the good ship's company,
Moses stuttering his firm
determination to go
eastward back to Eden,
Jonah showing snapshots
of the one that got away,
big Nathan getting
back rubs from his
very nervous servants,
Peter, unfamiliar
with this larger ship,
but still a good man
with a net and sail,
and Paul who's had his
share of shipwrecks,
Linus, Cletus, Clement,
Sixtus on the canon,
mother Miriam, her
eagle-eye and undemanding

heart attracting oh
what winds and fair,
Felicity, Perpetua,
black sisters dancing
pretty to a penny whistle,
me and you and San Diego
with a patch over one eye,

and Christ, the Commodore,
talking of booty, bounty,
somewhere there where
sun meets earth, adventure
and new birth, a launching
like no other and
we're well away.

*

This birth goes bang
like the one that rang
out in heaven when
God first looked and saw
God's Loveliness, let go
a Gasp, oh generations
ago, spewed elements
and gasses, broke out
in mountains, shook
forth trees that seek
out the sky, spit suns
for six days and
nights, howled hairy
animals, whistled

3

screeching notes that,
turning into birds,
took wing, squeezed
rocks tight, drooled
rivers, sweat noticeably
and, being so inspired,
scribbled out a Plan
furiously—a man
chasing a nimble woman
round a garden of
delights in anticipation
of more of this
Loveliness.

*

But in our sour way
we wouldn't play,
would rather market
fig leaves, very cheap,
don't mind the built-in
obsolescence,
everyone is wearing
them this year.
We slipped a troubling
doubt in God's mind
about good and evil,
maybe they began with
God, not with us.
We ran from death like
scorpions, begged God
to bring us out of

†

many Egypts. In our
hissing envy, we made God
surrender Loveliness
and pay a king's ransom
for a moment of our time.

Which God did
gladly do
in wonderful confusion,
Jesus Christ,
our ugliness limned
large, a sack of old
rags on his back,
dented pots and twigs to
light a fire on the earth
and cook his cold beans.
Just so, he fell
among thieves, hard,
struck down in the
turreted shadows of
worldly power. But
with a great heart-burst,
an almighty thirst,
a good word for everyone,
thanking and praising
at the end, our
Loveliness now
returned to God.

5

†

*

This is no rah rah
freshman rush, no
hazy intimation,
blooding, spells and
incantation, nothing
like they call these
days, initiation.

It's not so
personal or intimate
that Christ can't speak
of what's-his-name,
the third one from the
left with the suspenders
holding the kid who
just burped in its bib,
or ask the lady
with the hat to watch
her wax that's dripping
on her neighbor's
party dress.

This is for real,
for unimagined weal,
that when we're dead,
we stink, God lifts us
from the ocean floor,
belays our sins and
salvages our bones
and flesh, including
the suspenders that

we died in and the hat,
the hat for sure.

*

In this gifting
of the water, we gasp
God now, fix
steadfastly on God's
majestic spout
that races on before
our plunging mast,
Christ's standard
billowing above,
and pray that after
many ports of call
and many heaving
suns, land loom
at last and anchorage.

Spirit All Around

Whirlwind and gale,
in its fury, its impotent
wanting,
the hurricane heart
sweeps worldward
leveling all in its path,
like a parent who
loves too much,
hurts in the very gifting.

Raw stumps of lives,
jagged edges
of people, disfigured and
grim, oh,
the landscape left there,
cities in shambles,
dismay on the barren fields,
sunlight forgotten
and no surviving
in those high winds.

Eye of the storm
now, the stillness
within, and the heart's
sudden fear
at the deadfall,
like a child
finding no one at home,
only shadows in mirrors
and doors framed with menace
and lampshades staring.

Too many questions in sequence,
the melt-down
of every mind, riddles
with no solution, doubt
like a bat shrieking
soundlessly, pride
with an ax in its hand,
and there's no way out of this
no-man's land.

Blow, warming Spirit,
more mightily, sweep
through the ice-covered
caverns of this rock heart,
let daffodils burst
from its shrivelled
defiles so deep, so
sore, always in need
of more, more
is your name.

*

It starts out in knickers
and celluloid collars,
in taffeta dresses and
bows in your hair, and
the proud patent leather
smiles on your shoes
as you tiptoe on rose
petals down the beaming
aisle, how you look

†

like your mother and
father in better days,
your carriage straight
and still lest you spill
all you hold in your
head of the creed and
commandments, one after
the other you follow
those walking before you
for centuries, you
foreswear the perfumes
and the chafings of
your billowing lust
that is just beginning,
but you have no fear,
for the Spirit, from way
up in heaven, can land
on a dime down here
and stamp you with virtues
for every occasion,
like sparkling sequins
on your soul, make you
shine before astonished
angels, so when the bishop's
bony hands press God
into your skull, fold
earnestly around your cheeks
and skim your brow,
you do not flinch,
and when he's washed
the pomade from his hands,
a scent of lemon lingers
in the Mass afterwards.

*

Or can we Christ so
easily? For he
by that same Spirit
buffeted, that bellows,
let out unnatural groans
and sighs and grievous
sobbing at all sickening
pretense, bloated
vanity, imprisonings
and violent deprivation,
even at death, that thief.

He entered a conspiracy
with us, bade us
come and see
with unrelenting eyes
the world we live in
how it could be,
is, a garden of delights
when confirmation comes
from above, from God's
love, and as he broke
the waters of the Jordan
like a spearfish wet
and sleek, the Spirit dove
and dipped its wings
in quivering salute.

But first the testing,
vultures perched

†

along the desert rim
in hopes of his flesh
to eat, while down
below, the devil spat
and pawed the ground
and threw him three
high hard ones, and he
stroked them all
in leaping arcs over
the world's wall,
leaving no doubt about
his intentions.

He parried custom,
bridled at propriety,
not like an unsure
child who tests
itself against
a parent's frown
and needs to whittle
down all achievement
save its own,
but like a snow
leopard pacing
in a cage, he would be
free, unleashed in
charity to stalk
this loveless world.

He argued like a shrike
about God's whereabouts,
if God were still

†

to come, had passed
this way before,
or was even
now at the door
with a lop-sided smile
and a spiel, hawking
happiness.

And then the time he
blew right through
a man's head and a demon,
flushed, flew out
the other side
with a few parting remarks
about his ancestry,
and the man grinned
like he had been
to the dentist.

In a garden near
the riven tree of life
the Spirit made him feel
at once the gathered
wrath of ordinary
human beings that bursts
in livid judgment
on a God who dares
to rain and shine
on saints and sinners
equally, how he sweat
that one.

†

And finally, delirium
upon a cross a crazy
thought that trickles
like a droplet of blood
into his blasted brain
how can he eat this
endless shit
without a napkin
with his hands
nailed why are no
flowers growing
from this spear,
he let go
such a gasp his face
drained
blue
and he died.

*

Like a morning stillness
hung on rooftops
streaked by the new sun,
like a spire
framed against the surging
sky, like a sense
of something missing before
the first breeze stirs
or greeness grows
bright on the trees,
Jesus lay there in his tomb,
and the Spirit, Tongue

†

of Fire, placed
a reverent kiss upon
his lips, eternal gratitude,
unfeigned concern,
yes, respiration,
tendering. No force could
hold the Spirit back
and, like it dawning suddenly
upon a drowsy man
his children planned a picnic
for that very day, Jesus
jumped up.

*

Even now
the Spirit fills
this broken body,
Church, makes supple
ancient sinews, stretches
hearts and wills grown
atrophied, shakes
stupor from the mind, pries
open eyes, lets dry
tongues speak, massages
memory, lends tone
and feeling to the whole,
that we do likewise
to the next poor joker
comes along.

†

But all within
is ghostly, like a guest
I never see, who could
be me, of my mien and
temperament, or could
be who? speaking
my lines, weeping
for me, laughing
louder than me, making
my cause, housed
somewhere in my halls,
tabled with me
silently, turning me
temple while I sleep,
ictus or incubus I
cannot say, the trace of
incense when I wake,
a name I almost know,
like mine, that makes
me want to go
do something, but more
a calling out in
unfamiliar accents,
Abba, Jesus,
brother, sister.

More Than Love

What shall we say that's
fitting at this crossroads
of young love? Their
meeting here is not
the first. The summer
sky was often their
cathedral, shouldering
above them like the waves
that washed away their
cares. They celebrated
dreamy liturgies of
spring and genuflected
wantonly in winter
snows, their hymn of
laughter echoing against
the tree-lined slopes.
They posed in photographs
like saints in gothic
windows frozen in a
blast of autumn
sun. They went on
pilgrimage to visit
relatives and other
shrines, to make the
proper offering there.
They stood like stone-eyed
statues on the subway
car that carried them
from work and recognized
each other's features

†

in the breaking of
the bread at favorite
restaurants set back
from the world. By
vigil light they sipped
the cup of memory,
they whispered hope
and pictured children
tugging at their lives
impatiently. They shrove
each other from their
timid sins and sprinkled
benediction on each
other's brow like some
fat monk preparing for
the feast to come. They
are no novices to love.

*

And yet, would we be
wrong to raise a warning
cry and tell them every
love but love of God
must be transformed
or die? Would fiercely
costumed honor-guard
erect a solid wall of
silk and ruffles round
them to protect
them from from such
pointed news? Would rank

on rank of startled
worshippers, beginning
with their families,
rise to protest all
this suffocating talk
of God at such
a sacred moment?

Even pagans, mind you,
tell us marriage is
like dying. People
seldom dress so well
except at funerals
of presidents and kings.
In marriage
other people get
to read your almost
thoughts from almost
gestures, almost
words. You learn
to conjugate
life differently, no
more beginning with
first person singular.
Your souls are like
an iron-works where
choice is forged from
earth and flame, you
peer through masks at
one another's sweating
concentration, gesture

†

stiffly to the common task,
and punch your time
on clocks that count out
pain. A marriage takes
a couple to the brink
of love where wingless
they must fly or fall
like Lucifer in spirals
from on high, his proud
angelic cry diminishing
forever in its wake.

*

Whatever pagans say
or do, this Christian
matrimony is not marriage.
that's the difference
Jesus makes. He's
not just one of
the musicians playing
down to everybody's
funny way of dancing.
He's not the caterer
obsequious to every
taste. He's no magician
hired by the house
to work the water-jugs,
no three-card mountebank
who knows the heart's

position in advance.
He is in love himself.

He spoke about the love
of God as though it were
a date he was on once
before the world began.
His life was reminiscence
of those days, his death
a kind of rendevous
with God. The interval
was not just killing
time. He sought out
God along the way as if
he hoped to recognize
God in a crowd some day,
find Godprints in the salt
flats by the sea or be
so lucky that some people
heard of God before,
the very one that he
had known, and kick that
one around a while.
He stayed in touch with
God, left messages in
prayer about his needs,
the latest news, or any
bits of information he
could use to bend events
more surely to his vision
of the Reign of God.

†

Like anyone in love,
he loved the the world
entirely. Not even Adam
whooping at the creation
all around him, all,
could marvel more. So
drunk with love of God
was Jesus that he called
himself familiarly,
the groom, and sun-scorched
fishermen would giggle
nervously, could he mean
us? He seemed, at least,
a rare exception to
the priestly rule, that
people let you touch
their sicknesses but not
their joys, as though
you'd bring bad luck
because the power in you
works both ways.

*

Oh, there were voices
in the crowd, some
sour looks and
eyebrows raised like
pavillions here and there,
the occasional hard
stare, incomprehension

†

shrewdly deployed,
a kind of jut-jawed
innocence, sincerity
hefted like a truncheon,
the tell-tale
silences, on the mark
a concerted show
of neighborliness
and mutual concern,
indignant questions
passed along on unmoving
lips the way prisoners
speak: was he just
a butterfly too
shy to light
one place for long,
was there some story
with his parents,
did he hear his mother
whisper something
in the other room,
did he sense an
overearnestness
in his father's
conversation, was he
too keen to rule
out marriage in the world
to come, did he realize
how much he talked
of children, knew
their ways well,
did he never want

†

surcease from words
and more words,
was he afraid to lean,
to find another person
doesn't always fit
like a glove, was he
insinuating marriage
merely keeps the world
at bay, did he disdain
its privacy, make fun
of people waiting
for the appointed time
for sex to chime on
the hallway clock,
did he guffaw at
Adam's caveman act,
find Eve's largesse
a little overplayed,
was he unimpressed
by the opulence of
encompassing flesh,
did he prefer the
dark and adventurous
fringe, was he,
did he?

*

But if you saw him
climbing in the morning
darkness to his prayer,

†

if you met him at a well
one dry day, if you
watched him step across
to the whore's side,
felt his strong hand
guide a cripple's
first halting steps,
if you heard him reach
gamely for the next
persuasive phrase,
if you saw him clap
an enemy on the back,
if you listened to him
laugh like a sunburst
after rain or cry
without really knowing
why or needing to, if,
one journey's end,
you saw him break
and run on sharp
rocks with his young
stride to the margin of
a hill, look down
at last on Jerusalem,
his loose and painted
bride, if you knew his
innocence, you would not
begrudge him love.

He gathered, gathers
lovers in his train,

†

their hair festooned
with flowers, ribbons
trailing gaily
from their waist-bands,
grapes crushed
red upon their cheeks,
and leads them forth
to festival with God.

No Bright Shield

A table ringed
with high-backed chairs
where guests sit
motionless
in the uncertain
light from lampstands
nodding on the
rough-hewn walls,
and in the vaulted hollow
of that banquet hall
politely listen
to the tale each tells

of ancestry,
like a delicate lace,
fine woven
lines in patterns
they can barely trace
now, can only smoothe
with their finger tips
the wrinkles
left by time,

of travels
through the world
when it was young,
before their song
was hardly sung,
how they gazed
uncomprehending

†

at its panelled .
sights like tapestries
without familiar
characters or any plot
they could espy,

of reaching out
to life like raw
meat on a plank
that drips with
blood and spice,
how they gorged
their appetite,

of loves
like reddest wine
from bursting
vines entwined
deliciously
in the autumn heat,
how they drank it
to exhaustion down
to the bitter marc,

of faces
that they wore for
various occasions,
shaped so
conveniently like
melting wax from
stately candlesticks,

of ambition
most perilous,
like a fragile goblet spun
from glass, transparent
at the last,

of plans
set out like shining
silverware
in a row,

of thoughts,
like kitchen flies,
that darted
here and there
for tiny scraps
of truth

of mysteries
they tried to break
like walnuts
with their teeth,

of illusions
that they peeled away
like rind,

of hopes
like bitter seeds
they had to spit out
in their hand.

†

And when the circle
is complete,
all gather silence
round them
like a cloak against
the raw night air
and stare
with fatal sympathy
into the last light,
no word of thanks
being uttered
ever at this banquet
of the dead.

*

Yet thanking is a
simple art, a rippling
shudder in the womb
at our first taste of
flesh and blood, a
quickening of wide-eyed
possibility at the
proffered breast, a
pleasant squirming when
a smile descends
on us, a bursting
expectation when
we're lifted up,
a languid satisfaction
at being bathed by hand,
a flush of royalty

†

as we are dressed,
surprise expanding
in our breast
with each new shining
object in our lives,
a goodness all
over us, the omen
of a time to come,
a cycle taken up,
when lovers give
their very bodies
graciously for
one another's joy.

Until the unforgiving
consciousness of
need spoils everything,
sets up its dreary
dialectic, this for
that, intones its
epileptic litany
of rights, drapes itself
in robes of justice,
roots like a pig's snout
among its prerogatives,
keeps dreadful count
of favors done and
favors pending, gives
but to be given, bargains
like a sharp-eyed
peddler, claws for any
leverage, expects

†

blood on every altar,
in its tortured
offertory never feels
the loving in the giving
and will not say thanks.

*

Now Jesus, he was
different, in his other
life he grew up golden
far above this world,
would bicycle around
the galaxies, go
hiking in the
mounting clouds, slide
down solid winds,
race lumbering trains
of stars, poke
bubbles on the sun
with a long stick,
skim stones across
celestial oceans,
pantomine the faces on
the moon, shoot silver
arrows at the planets,
play in the streaming
tracts of light, make
magic music in his heart
to thank and praise
his Father's goodness.

Down here,
they told him,
life is no free
lunch, you have to
gouge it out of deserts,
suck it up from
the sea, pluck its fruits
from impossible trees—
it makes you hard,
and dangerous,
you wouldn't tell
a hungry man, be
grateful for the taste
of death.

He'd get the odd
exception, like
the lady once who
shined his shoes
with her mop
of voluptuous hair,
or the leper
who came back to ask him
would he need
some bandages slightly
used, or like the crazy
madman who kept
crying after him
what a great guy he was,
or when Zacchaeus
got expansive
after brandy and cigars,

†

or the colonel coming
stiffly to attention
when his little girl was cured,
or the *really* kind ones
who would change the subject
when he couldn't
seem to do a thing for them
and ask him how
his mother was and was
he still in the construction
business.

Others would just take
the gift and go
their way, like it wasn't
so, like he did
something dark and
intimate to them, got inside
their bodies, somehow
tampered with their
controls, they needed
distance was their phrase,
he never quite could
follow that.

*

It ended, sort of,
at a supper, one of those
family things where
love and hate sit
next to one another, people

work on the puzzle
of their lives,
discover words they never
meant the same by, share
a common language for
what can't be said,
produce with a flourish
new versions of themselves,
protest their histories,
agree upon the enemy,
unseal old briefs, expose
the heart's uncertainty,
reshape alliances and move
the whole thing
imperceptibly ahead.

Like a stallion blinded
by a canyon wall, like
a boxer with the strength
gone from his arms,
like an army with its
back against the sea,
like a mining man whose
cough is getting worse,
like a poor man's curse
who can't support his
family, it all was
closing in on him.

If Moses led a million
people out of Egypt,
got clear title to

†

the Promised Land, had
God's ways down cold
on stone, if David built
a sparkling city
to the skies and Solomon
was so wise he even
figured out the Queen
of Sheba, if every exile
made it back from Babylon,
it wouldn't help him now.

What good are covenants
when even one man dies,
plans fall apart,
they break your goddam
heart, the world's mistakes
keep catching up
and nothing to be done.

*

Out of the whirlwind
of these thoughts
he heard a voice,
his father, Joseph,
dreamer he was,
would think along
a grain of wood
with his hands while
he talked, feel
its texture, work out
its pliant strength,

†

take its inner worth.
A person is exposed,
he used to say,
by giving. Oh he may keep
to the formalities,
Take this, Take that,
but really means, or must,
himself—no other,
nothing substituting,
not his conviction
in a cause nor his
manifest authority,
not his patient endurance
nor even the piety
he may profess—but
himself, his being
in love. That's it.
No hedge around
his feelings,
no bright shield
against the fear
the gift may not
be there to give
some day.

He knew he now had
reached the sticking
point, that it is hard
to thank a God
whose gift to you
is that you give it
all away.

†

If he could just
do that, he could
be gracious
in his present pain,
be gentle when
the killing came.
Could do alright.
No airy inspiration came
to save him from this
choice. What moved
him were the people
in that room, their
histories wound
long and tight
with his like an oath,
faces that looked
toward him then looked
away, resolve that
waited on his own,
hopes pinned on him,
an honest desperation,
hunger, how could he
turn them down?

And catching his own
reflection in a
broken hourglass, he saw
there compassion,
dignity, great peace,
he saw at last he was
God's son,

who did not hate
him, loved him
faithfully, like him
was nourishment,
intoxication, pledge,
was with him
even now.

Like Job restored,
embracing all
his friends,
his enemies and
anyone at that point
who would just enjoy
a party, Jesus
raised a toast of thanks—
to life—that cracks
across the sky like
thunder to this day.

On The Mend

This jigsaw life,
pieces don't fit,
you turn them
this way, that
way, it comes out
half a face
here, almost
a tree there,
unconnected
sky, misshapen
windows (looking
out or in?),
what could be
an elegant hand
pointing to
a spider web,
unfinished
flowers in
what will be
a vase, the
small suggestion
of a woman's shoulder,
something like
embroidery
lying on the arm
of a couch with
no leg, a parrot
in mid air,
a stairway leading
somewhere, no
sound across the

†

broken spaces,
waiting
for what isn't
perhaps there.

So, who's to say
it should be
otherwise, that
there should be some
hope of wholeness,
of completion, like
the seventh morning
God got out of
bed, that was some
week, he said,
but now it all
looks pretty good.
We seem more suited
to distraction,
our trailing parts
clutched to our chests
like Kewpie dolls,
gawking at the barkers
on life's midway,
trying out the rides,
our faces stuffed
with cotton
candy, laughing
at the freaks who
mimic us, keeping time
to a calliope, until
the bus leaves

†

and even death is just
the next thing
on the list.

Yet we danced
with death
before, on this
very floor, only
she wore a different
outfit then, did
her hair another
way, we could tell
her perfume, the same
brocaded purse, she
called herself
plague,
addiction,
cancer,
madness,
trauma,
stroke,
morbidity,
we felt her close
to us, she kept
good time,
used little phrases
we would guess
were french or
something, said
she knew a lot
of people here
and there, she

†

always smiled
but never looked
right at us, never
flattered us,
and when the band
broke, she sat alone
and moved her fan
back and forth
across her delicate
neck, her drink
untouched, just
seemed to wait for
the next dance
to begin.

*

Welcome, then,
to the Eschatological
College of Healing
Knowledge and Bodily
Restoration, unLtd.,
where we dissect
all matters pertinent,
probe the arcane
crafts and methods used
to get the suckers
up and around again,
dispense the mysteries,
proscribe an alchemy of
eternal love, of fiddling

†

around inside and other
time-worn remedies.

Some say the body
holds the spirit
up like a corset,
is its eyes and ears,
displays its moods,
points it to its prey,
retrieves what
the spirit desires and
gets pittance in return,
in fact is ridiculed,
because the spirit
thinks that it's
hot stuff, wants
everything all
at once and cannot
stand the body's
ponderous delay.

But others say
the spirit is the body's
friend, takes it
everywhere, dresses
it up, introduces it
around, makes a name
for it, conceals
its unseemly parts,
abides its nervous
schedules, gets it to
laugh, keeps the noise

†

down while the body
sleeps.

The healer plays
the diplomat in this
dispute, holds
meetings separately
with each lest
righteous tempers
prevail, attends to
each as if there
were no other
for the moment, rarely
speaks ill of either
in the other's presence
unless of course that
helps, smiles vaguely
at jokes that might
offend, creates
occasions where the
body and the spirit
can pretend
to work together
without losing face,
sees nothing
artificial in this,
nothing cynical, if
it but heal *something*.

The healer knows
well the enemy, its
droppings carry

†

doom, its howl
is from old,
its practised teeth
swivel back and forth
with its rapacious
eyes, its orgasm
is to extend its claws,
its preferred way
is gradual
mutilation.

The healer stays
in tune with nature,
stretches pain out
like a redness spread
so low and wide
along the earth's
caked rim the sun's
intensity subsides,
gets bitter memories
to spend themselves like
repetitious waves upon
the accepting shore,
displays the mind's
confusion like fish
in an aquarium, each
stinging question,
each wall-eyed
doubt and tentacled
decision swimming
in and out of
the dark waters

now a distinct beauty
and surprise,
reduces spasms
of remorse like a
wrangler playing out
rope to a wild horse,
stirs up stagnant
pools of depression
and despair like
a silvery freshet
leaping down
a mountain face.

The healer takes
complaints in stride,
The bloody thing
still doesn't work,
there's something
still inside, the
bandage is too wide
for my personality,
I'll keep the crutches
all the same, this is
some sort of game, don't
poke me in the eye.
The healer learns
to sigh a lot, which
people read as something
deep but simply may
mean, bye-bye.

†

The only time
you think you really
might have
healed someone
is when you feel
deflated, like you
were punched in
the chest, or you feel
exposed and your nerve
starts to go, like
something is slightly
behind you to your left,
in your blind spot,
a silence bound up with
your name, something
owed, some code
violated, some claim
unsubstantiated,
like faded writing
on soft stone, in
Latin most likely
but it doesn't matter,
and that is strangely
why you are both
confident and afraid.

*

Ah Christ,
don't unpeel my eyes
then press me about
what I want to see,

†

don't unsling my limbs
expecting me to walk
a straight and narrow
line, don't stem the rot
in me then offer me
some antiseptic future,
don't ream my ears
just to give me uplifting
speeches, don't play
to the crowds at my
expense, don't spare me
only on condition,
don't you see, I feel
my wholeness is me —
what I want now —
cure me rather of THAT.

Jesus didn't hesitate
but set his amulets and
scalpel on the ground,
drew his black cape high
across his tearful face,
at first I thought me
to embrace, then
simply stepped aside
and let in such a blast
of God as made my buttocks
jump, my hair shoot
out stiff from my head,
my nostrils blow like
freight-trains in a tunnel,
my bones click like dice,

†

my heart pinwheel
in place, a cold
grace come over me,
a kind of sympathy
for the world, for
its relentless dying,
mine no less, that
lifted me from my
distress, not magically
but making me more
brave, like a traveller
setting out for
scarred hills high
in the distance I step
up the pace now
to reach the end, the
all, the One. Amen.

Righteous Day

Will they spot
the broken fishook
in my mouth, trace
the doctored brand
on my flanks, recognize
the familiar odor,
hear the spastic tap
of my foot on the floor?

Better sit it out,
grin my innocent monkey
grin into the lights,
let them search
behind my cooperative
squint for shouting
clues, watch my
judges weary, peel off
their suspenders,
splash water on their
faces, take their
turn at the card
game in the other room.

It's all interrogation
in the end, someone
with a list, some
fact you supposedly
missed, an elegant web
of inference, then
a burst of silence,

†

the slab-like hand
on your shoulder,
victorious glances
you're not part of,
they pile their papers
before them like fine
linen, that's it,
they say.

If they only knew
the half of it. My
darkness is brighter
than their lights,
my evil is old
like swamp trees,
my eye bulges
when it remembers,
I reach the skies
with my braying,
my pride heaves
like entrails
exposed, I prefer
the wandering
sewers, my lust
is tireless pursuit,
I love to laugh
my enemies into their
graves, I thrive
on their panic,
how I hate all
that is neat and good.

†

*

The Lord God crouched
behind a tree
to see this marvel, man,
with his preposterous
fig leaf and slouched
hat, his uncontrollable
drool, the erratic
speeches made to
basically uninterested
birds and cattle too
polite to walk away,
the posturing and
unsubstantial threats,
a pup playing at warrior.

Why, the Lord God
could hit angels
from a thousand meters
with His blow-gun,
even sideways, could
prick Leviathan
like a fat bubble,
hold down hot
geysers with His elbow,
could balance on vines
as thin as spaghetti,
could find
the kingfisher's eggs
without any help
of a map.

†

I swear, the Lord God
said, this has to stop,
the man could hurt
himself not to mention
his watery seed;
the woman waving her jug
of cider wantonly
from the distant crag
could fall and miss
the soft pine-beds
below, the only
question is should I
go myself or send
someone?

*

When judgment comes
down, people run
as if to see an accident
at the corner, brake
reverently at
the scene, fix
first on the ensemble,
who else is there,
what they wear and
how they look,
saving the victim
for last, savoring
the victim, this icon
of themselves, a body
in the gutter, sticky

†

candy wrappers floating
there on water mixed
with blood, they exchange
impressions of what
happened, reenact in the
slow-motion of the mind
the sequence of terror
and pain, edify one
another with recollected
tales of equal horror,
lucky for them it
wasn't their turn.

When judgment comes
down, people lament
the system, how the odds
are stacked against you,
you can never figure
who's in charge,
if only others did
their job, you say,
the way it always goes
around and comes back,
instructions don't
add up and strangers
get the credit, time
is always running out.

When judgment comes
down, it's a blinding
day, the blue
of the sky smacking

†

rooftops, wires
streaking from telephone
poles, trees
unlimbering from the
stiff sentinel of night,
a dog showing off
for its breakfast,
people sinking
back deliciously
under the blankets,
bikes in the front
yards ready
for serious play,
stores half open and bang.

*

Jesus laughed,
at first just
high in his cheekbones,
his nose pinching
slightly at the top,
then a slushing
sound at the sides
of his tongue
as his cheeks rounded,
his tightened throat
sending air back
down his windpipe
to beat against
his ribs, rebound
with a whoosh, whirl

†

around inside him,
then a tickling, no
holding it, dizzy
escape now, upward
pressure slamming
his eyelids down,
his mouth stretched
out as far as it would
go, his nostrils
closed tight, teeth
pulled forward,
hysterical, precipitous
glee, shaking, yes, he
answered the dreary
man in the crowd
with a face
like an overripe squash,
will sinners get
their comeuppance?
(heeeeeeeee), will they
get their comeuppance?
(whaa-hooooooh),
yes, I guess
you could say that
(huuuaaaaaaaah).

The trick is to
remove the infectious
complaint without
offing the sinner,
for which you need
an image of yourself

†

as very small, almost
disappearing, yet
totally caressed
by God's softness,
like exotic fumes
from the Vap-O-Rub
on your chest when
you're sick or steaming
towels on your face
in the barbershop
or burrowing into your
mother's breasts after
the harvest is barned
or like the sweetly
exhausting end
of a pillow fight,
whatever makes you
less a menace, more
calm, more attuned to
the goodness fighting
its way out of
the sinner, looking
for a door, a chink,
an airshaft, anything
but the bedlam within.

Next you strike
up a conversation,
most circuitously
discuss the origin of
clouds, the cricket's
intent, how rain

†

gets its smell,
whether lines drawn
straight out from
our toes would be
parallel, that sort
of harmless thing,
but you keep your
focus on God's
belly button, know
your lifeline there,
how God takes care
with you, treats
you to creation like
so many luscious
watermelon, never
forces total clarity
on you and is not
bound by your heaven
and hell.

To be sure, you can
always chart the
elusive movements of
a lie as such, expose
the intricate circuitry
of pride in itself,
theorize about the sticky,
lumpish qualities of lust,
you can unearth for
the world's instruction
all the mutilated victims
ever of violence,

can analyze if you
wish the infuriating
pace of sloth, you can
fix the fatal point
at which no one turns
back from the pit, you
can lay open the
foul-smelling and effete
essence of greed, flay
ignorance for its general
willfulness, you can let
go broadsides at
any perversion you want,

but at that fragile
moment of forgiving,
remember how even
the unwieldy earth
steadies itself
lest it disturb the
spindly efforts of a
bird on its first ascent,
remember how the sun
holds back its
too terrible light
lest it startle
the waking child,
and when the sinner
cringes there before
you, remember just
this, you are looking
in a mirror, my friend.

†

They sent him packing
finally, his noise
too grating on their ears,
his hope too contradicted
by their lives, his love
a slap in their
collective face.
The cover-story spoke
of some disgrace, some
uncleanness he
incurred, remarks he made
that were overheard and
brought to the right places.
But on the night before
he died, a petty thief
who wouldn't give
his name but had, it
seems, no ax to grind
said he saw Jesus running
through the city
licking the doorposts
of the houses till
his tongue bled,
stopping occasionally
to bang his head on
a cart-wheel, stuffing
his pockets with excrement
everywhere, reading
frantic prayers over
the public wells and

†

shouting something down
the shuttered alleyways.
His friends then
found him, cleaned him
up and that was it,
except they say he
sat through the feast
wearing a queer smile
and when they asked
him he replied, sort
of triumphantly,
*I'm taking it all
with me.*

A Place Of His Own

Weathervane
wheeling
very slowly
over

the cobwebbed
barn with its
sagging, slate-gray
epaulettes,
dried out,
thornbushes
climbing too high up
its splintering sides,
the hay forgotten,
hornets
immobilized
by the cold,

anchored uncertainly
in the worn wood,
its iron arms
twisted at
some invisible forge,
patterns of rust
streaking it
like tears,
its blunted
finger pointing
unsteadily at
unkempt crows

sliding by
on some airborne
mission, nothing
gracious to it,
nothing sleek,
only an incongruous
appendage now to
the proud cock
that sits astride
it still.

> If it could
> but remember
> how the wind
> was once, how after
> unsparing rains
> the fields
> pushed up whole
> armies of victorious
> daffodils!

*

I worry, doctor,
in my head I mean

I parent someone else's child,

I rule where reason doesn't really count,

I temper what should be wild,

†

weigh out unfailing grace in small amounts,

I show the way to those who see,

remind those who seldom forget,

I wait on people who would pamper me,

command a pace others may freely set,

I lead where most have gone before,

I warn of dangers that pass all the same,

I gather nations but to divide them more,

I bless things in someone else's name,

I shepherd as though people could be sheep,

I cleanse stains from immaculate altars,

waken those who aren't asleep,

I strengthen those who never seem to falter,

predict events already history,

I guard a castle with no walls,

I claim to master mystery,

I hand down judgment in empty halls.

†

If my love
does such
innocent violence,
am I preaching
to my own
enormous silence?

*

The hell with him,
he said, prop his body
by that tree instead,
where someone with
more time than me
will find him, dig
his grave, throw in
some lime mixed with
the usual prayers.
He was your father.
So. I'm sorry, but
I have to go to
the other towns.
My brother is being
lynched there, lies
in some stinking
jail, blood on his
shirt-tail, can't speak
the lingo, down on
his luck, they found
some melons in his
truck that wasn't his
and wouldn't go

†

anyway. You know
how people are.
I need some back-up,
organized, before
they all get wise
and cut his throat
in his cell, dump
his body in a well
and gloat about it
afterwards at the
barbecue and dance.
You come right now,
we have a chance.
For, look, the sun
is dying on the
western wall,
we must cross
the shivering hills
this very night.

*

Along the way wild
beasts listened
from their lairs,
could tell his voice
was not theirs
because it was
mixed with stars.
I would have liked
a spread of land
myself, he said,

†

where I could grow
things down rows
I seeded with sunburned
hands, spade over
sod fat with worms,
taste the salt of my
sweat on my tongue,
clear my throat
for a solitary tune,
raise walls against
man-high winds, fix
things to last,
watch the blue of
the flame chew on
logs in my hearth,
be helped by a
good woman to get things
done and know better
why, rock back and
forth with the seasons
painted on my porch
screen, smile like a
great squat sun on
children of mine.
But I have always
feared the sameness
in the insect's eye,
that unmoving
stare so full of purpose
yet impassive to
the lush expanse
reflected on its

†

very surface.
Would I be so
narrowed? I was made
for mountains,
not for the repetitious
plain. I somehow
need to see how
the whole world would
be if there wasn't me
in it.

*

I hated priests,
who told me God
lived far away
and needed Death
for some improvements
he was doing on
his estates, so
send him bird-parts,
entrails, broken
hopes, medallions
of beef, racking
tears, bowls of pig's
blood, defeated
ambitions, voided
placentas, sour
memories, shiny
bones, declining
juices or anyting
else you can think of.

✝

Or God was so upset
by Sin he had to
take aspirin, have
angels fan his
four-poster bed with
their wings and pass
him kleenex.
At least they never
called *me* priest.

*

Sure I want to
speak, no, shout
for God, sing out all
I feel about God's
lavish unfolding,
filling, show
God off in albums,
every funny face
God made in history,
each alias assumed,
the horse-play and
grand-standing.
But my words come
out like buckling
skyscrapers, like
slow-moving mud,
like toothless
lawyers arguing,
like a curse poorly
put, a note slightly

†

off-key, like a protest
I don't quite mean,
like flailing at
unruffled routines.
My mouth is crammed
with religion,
people hunkering
down, contorted,
writhing, one long
pitiful sniffle,
one continuous
whine, yet hiding
the half of their
truth that looks
at its wristwatch and
calculates,
that has no faith,
that won't let itself
be hooked like
a wide-eyed child
by outlandish promises.

*

My God sits
high in the soul's
towers to catch the
sun with bare chest,
halloes the distant
hills, exultant,
laughs from the
parapets, peeks

†

through loop-holes at
the motley strolling
past the barbican,
builds great fires
in the keep to turn
the meat and mull
wine from the
grinning casks, has
instruments to hand
for madrigals and
galops, starts
an infectious roar
through the thick
stone walls around.

*

But that's just
Kingdom talk.
Reality is you
people and me doing
good where we can,
always with a plan,
not too much tied
to who's-in-charge
and games like that
but leaving God's
love here and there
like smoke-pots
against the world's
chill or cats'
eyes on a dark

stretch of highway
or even harsh
stones underfoot
that remind.
We beacon God
from stark, sheer
headlands, tell
people steer this way
if they dare, follow in
on our prayer and
sweet fasting.

*

The ordination took
place anyway. They
threw a purple
chasuble on top
his seamless alb,
cinctured him extra
tight, made a mitre
out of thorns, gave
him his own words
to eat, his blood to
lick from his swollen
lip, had him prostrate
in the aisle between
the cheering crowds,
led him in procession
to the altar shaped
like a streamlined
skull, anointed his
palms to the exact

†

spot, made him swear
obedience to Death,
inscribed his name
smartly on a shingle,
elevated him to a
rickety pulpit, fixed
him for good, full
stipend for all
his simplicity.

*

Ah, woe is me, he said,
no angels for me now.
I see but blood-red
sky, my last, nor know how
to bid this lovely earth
farewell, such pain
inhabits me and puts my worth
in doubt. He asked again,
where does love go
when passion ends? No
voice responded from above,
no confirmatory dove
descended on his head.
Enough that I am dead,
he cried, if that's the price.
It's no great sacrifice
for me to go back home
where friends can come
one day when the world bends
out of time, ends
on a graceful sigh,
and what high jinks then!

About the Author

George McCauley is a New York born and based Jesuit priest who has been a teacher of theology.